RUN FREE

RUN FREE

SHORT BUT GRIPPING

S. BANNERWAY

This is a work of fiction. Names, characters, places, and incidents either are the product of the author's imagination or are used fictitiously. Any resemblance to actual persons, living or dead, events, or locales is entirely coincidental.

First paperback edition 2023

Book design by PublishingPush

978-1-80541-107-9 (Paperback)
978-1-80541-108-6 (eBook)

In loving memory of Michael Orchard,
A husband, a father and my hero.
25 July 1942–17 July 2021

CHAPTER 1

Dawn lasered through the curtains where Richard Gartner lay on his back in bed, wide awake, staring at the ceiling. His mind raced over the day ahead. He took a deep breath. 'It's going to be a difficult day'.

As a sergeant in an elite team within the British Army, Richard's twenty years of service had seen him deployed in conflicts around the world: Africa, Afghanistan, Iraq. Today, he was going to Cape Town for six months, fighting with the South African militia against a feared uprising among rebel troops.

The daylight grew stronger. Richard's wife, Lisa, woke up and stretched under the duvet, looking across to see him already awake. She rolled over and cuddled up, then hugged him tight, a sign to say 'It'll be OK'.

He kissed her forehead and whispered, 'I know, my love'.

They had been married for twenty-four years. Childhood sweethearts at school, their eyes had never wandered from each other since then. Lisa was everything he had ever wanted or needed, calling her his 'perfect princess'.

Lisa knew the routine after so many years. She had been there for the highs – when he was awarded medals for long service, active service, high gallantry, bravery – but also the lows – long periods without speaking after Richard's friends had been killed while on active service.

Now, they enjoyed the brief bliss of this moment together, knowing it would soon be the end of the lows: Richard would retire after this deployment. They looked forward to their lives being about them for a change, and what they wanted to do together.

Richard got up and went for a shower while Lisa put on her dressing gown and went downstairs to make coffee. Flicking on the kettle, she paused, leaning against the kitchen worktop for support, and gave a small cry. She quickly masked her mouth to muffle the sound, tears running down her face. She had to pull herself together, to not show Richard she was struggling. She wiped her face, blew her nose and shook her head as though shaking away the sad thoughts.

Richard came downstairs wearing hiking trousers, T-shirt and walking boots. His clothes hadn't changed style in twenty four years. He wasn't interested in new clothes, hairstyles or the latest phone. He had what he wanted, and that was enough. Grabbing the mug of coffee Lisa had made for him, he sat opposite her at the kitchen table and reached for her hands across its cold marble surface.

'If anything happens, you know the score', Richard said.

Lisa nodded.

'Just do what you've always done and come home safe to me', she replied.

He looked at the clock on the wall, 'Well, perfect princess, time I was going'.

He grabbed his bag from the hallway and opened the front door. Lisa threw her arms around his neck, squeezing so tightly that he nearly lost his footing. He wrapped his arms around her, snuffling her neck, her hair over his face. The scent of her shampoo would always remind him of home.

'Love you so much. I'll be back soon. Promise'.

They separated reluctantly from their embrace, Lisa holding on to him as long as possible. He walked towards his car, threw his bag in the back and climbed into the driver's seat. He couldn't look at her, he knew it would break the seal, causing emotions which he hated showing. Reversing down the drive, wheels crunching on gravel, he reached the road and shifted into first gear. He glanced back to see Lisa leaning against the door frame, raised a hand to wave goodbye, then accelerated down the narrow lane.

She waved back, mouthing, 'Love you' as he disappeared from sight.

While driving the thirty-five miles to work, Richard had snapped out of home mode and into that of a soldier – alert and aware at all times. Arriving at the gates of his barracks, he showed his ID to security and headed towards the car park where his car would stay for the entire deployment. He chose a parking space at the end of a row, with a large space around it, so that neither people nor trees would damage the car. He was very particular about small details, one of the reasons why his military career had been successful. He threw his bag over his shoulder and walked towards his office, locking the car as he went. The bleeping lock code echoed across the quiet camp.

Using his personal key code, Richard opened his office door. All he had to do was grab his pre-packed deployment bag and call the transport department for an 6:30am hours pick-up for the airport next day.

CHAPTER 2

The car arrived outside Richard's office at 6:30am hours sharp. His flight, two hours' drive from camp, was direct to Cape Town. He loaded his deployment bag into the car and climbed in. The young driver looked at him. 'Are you ready to go, Sergeant?' Richard raised a hand and leaned forward as an order to advance. The journey to the airport was filled with phone calls to South Africa; mainly updates from Richard's boss on recent enemy activity, letting Richard know what to expect when he arrived.

In the airport lounge, with a coffee and a sandwich, his bag checked in, waiting for his gate to be called, a feeling of guilt crept over him. He usually felt this, going to work while leaving Lisa at home. He closed his eyes tight and held them shut for a few seconds to blank the feeling. His love for Lisa was vast, but as a professional soldier he knew that his mind had to be in the game, on the job.

He glanced at the departure screens, looking for flight BA299 to Cape Town, but also searched through the flights of holiday destinations – where would it be lovely to take Lisa when he returned? They tried to holiday at least once a year; enjoying the scenery, trying new adventures, eating the local food, but mostly just spending time together. He noticed Cuba as a destination.

'Sold. That's where we're going next'.

Lisa had mentioned Cuba a few years ago, but they had never got around to booking anything. He would keep this one as a surprise, a celebratory treat for her after his last tour of duty.

Thirty minutes later, he heard the announcement: 'Cape Town South Africa, departure gate forty-three, boarding now'. The airport was surprisingly busy for a Tuesday in mid-April, people weaving amongst themselves like worker ants collecting forage. He boarded the British Airways plane into business class and settled down for the eight-hour flight. Opening his phone with its wallpaper of Lisa and him on a beach at sunset, he sent a last text to her:

'On the plane now, will call from SA. Love you more than anything in this world, perfect princess'.

After pressing send, he changed the wallpaper to a default image of a sunflower. He did this every time he deployed so that, if ever he were taken prisoner, the enemy would not know what Lisa looked like, or even if she existed.

He leaned back into the soft seat, feet propped up and eye mask on. He was asleep in seconds. Today's early morning rush, and leaving Lisa yesterday, had tired him out. When he awoke and glanced out the small rectangular window, they were already over Africa with only three hours to go. Eating and reading soon passed the time. Looking out, he recognised the landscape as the plane descended into Cape Town airport.

Richard grabbed his bag from the luggage carousel and made his way through the airport, scanning the crowd for a familiar face to meet him. Taxi drivers called out 'Taxi, sir, taxi, boss', each one eager for business. They wore old combat shorts, grubby T-shirts and trainers that looked as though they had been passed down through generations.

The airport smelled strongly of bodies and cheap aftershave. Heat blasted in through large open windows, the air conditioning struggling to control the temperature. Even at dusk at 8:30pm, it was still twenty-seven degrees. People ran from door to door with their baggage, couples cuddled their newly arrived friends and family.

Richard walked past the line of keen taxi drivers until he recognised someone in the crowd. Shaved head, a beard with patches of grey, heavy muscular build and stern face, dust-covered trousers, a blue-and-white checked shirt with the sleeves rolled up. Dave.

Dave was Richard's work partner. He had already been in South Africa for a month, setting up contacts and areas for work. They greeted each other with a firm handshake and a heavy slap on the shoulder. They had been mates for years, and had a great deal of respect for each other.

A tough-speaking cockney, Dave had been in the forces since he was sixteen. It had shaped him into a hard character who was lonely away from his work. Single, never married, too busy travelling, and no women ever hung around very long when he was on leave. Drink had always been his problem, it got the better of him when he was off duty. Dave always wondered how Richard managed to do his job and return to a happy home life. Richard knew that most of Dave's problems stemmed from an incident eight years earlier when he was injured by a suicide bomber – a scar down the left side of his face and a skin graft on his left arm.

Dave slung Richard's bag over his shoulder and led him outside to a white 4x4 Mitsubishi Shogun armoured car. They drove out of the airport, straight into the hectic traffic, beeping horns and random shouts, people scurrying everywhere. Cape Town was a bustling city, even in the late hours. Richard watched the locals go about their evening routine: middle-aged men in suits travelling from work, briefcases in hand, baggy-eyed, with ties pulled away from their neck, top buttons undone; women braiding hair on benches along the street, with tourists queuing to get a new style on the cheap. Busy corner shops sold fruit and vegetables in baskets piled high, so full they would surely collapse. Bus stops and bicycles appeared at every turn of the road.

'What a crazy city, no order anywhere', Richard thought.

Towards the city limits there were fewer street-lights, brick houses became metal, tarmac roads became gravel. Dave now drove as though he were drunk, swerving left and right to avoid half-metre sized pot holes. The sound of tyres on gravel reminded Richard of pulling into his drive at home – if only that were the case – but it reminded him he should let Lisa know he was safe: 'In SA now, with Dave on way to camp. All OK. Hope you had a good day. Love you xx'.

Dave looked across. 'Everything all right with the wife, Ginge?'

Ginge was Richard's nickname. He would get patches of ginger hair whenever he grew a beard. With a small grin, he replied.

'Yeah. All good mate. Last time, then that's it for me'.

'You'll miss this madness, you know you will', Dave chuckled.

Richard looked out into the pitch darkness of the South African night. Only the faint outline of trees could be seen.

'Trust me, no more than I'm missing her now'.

The outpost was a one-storey brick house inside a tall brick wall. After Richard and Dave drove into the compound, the double gates, made of metal, were secured shut with a heavy chain and padlock. This was the heart of militia territory. Dave showed Richard to his room, a small corner one with a single bed and mirror, the ceiling only slightly higher than the top of his head. One light bulb hung from the middle of the room, flickering like a disco ball. It didn't take him long to unpack and throw on a fresh T-shirt.

The familiar London accent bellowed down the corridor.

'Mate, when you're ready, he's in his office.

Dave was referring to their Officer-in-Command on the ground, Major Nixon. He led Richard across the courtyard to a small outbuilding.

The Major stood up behind his desk as they walked in and held out his hand.

'Good to see you out here, Rich, we've been busy'.

Richard grasped his hand, shook it tight. There was a great amount of respect in the room. Richard respected his boss; you don't get to be Major easily. Richard was respected for the work and actions he had done over the years. Being awarded one medal for bravery was an achievement, but two was unheard of.

'Good to be here, Sir. What's the plan and when do we go out again?' Richard asked.

Major Nixon sat down, leaning back in his big leather chair.

'Get some sleep mate, and we'll get a plan together tomorrow'.

Richard gave a nod in acknowledgment.

Back in his room, he unpacked properly, showered, climbed into bed. The bedsprings pushed into his back through the thin mattress. The fan whirred from side to side on full power. He opened his phone and saw Lisa's message.

'Glad you arrived OK. Day OK, work busy. Love you too, call whenever you can xx'.

He closed the phone and laid his head on the pillow, drifting off to sounds of the lads in the communications sending radio checks to ground patrols.

CHAPTER 3

Lisa drove through winding country lanes. The traffic was light and the sun was breaking through gaps in the clouds. She was listening to chilled Sunday music on the radio, but her excitement was like a volcano about to erupt. She arrived in a small, quiet village in the depths of Dorset and turned into a long drive with tall hedges on each side. A large manor house loomed at the end of the drive, behind double wooden gates. Lisa parked in a small space outside and gathered her bag, giggling to herself. She knew this would change her and Richard's life for the better. As she approached the house, she heard yelps and barks. Excitement was getting the better of her. Before she reached the front door, the owner appeared around the corner.

'You must be Lisa', a friendly voice said. 'Great! I'm Michelle, please come and see the little critters'.

Michelle was in her mid-fifties, short and plump, with a friendly, ruddy face and huge smile. She was dressed in jeans and a dirty T-shirt while cleaning up after the puppies. Her eyes looked tired, but she was happy to see Lisa.

Lisa skipped a little as she followed Michelle round the corner of the house. They went through the back door into an old-fashioned, country-style kitchen painted cream, with a tiled floor. The smell of dog hit Lisa instantly. The room was filled with the sound of six puppies crying for attention and their mother's milk. A three-foot-high wooden pen stood in the corner. Lisa leaned over and her eyes widened with joy. The mother lay on her side, looking worn out, while six golden retriever puppies climbed over each other, fighting for a suckle. They were like golden balls of fur, with coats too long for their bodies. Their legs collapsed as they tried to walk for the first time, eyes trying to grasp what was going on around them. The mother lifted her head slightly while Lisa stared into the pen, then laid her head down with sheer fatigue.

'Cute, huh?', Michelle claimed proudly.

'Unbelievably! Richard will be so thrilled when he's back home'.

‘Is it a surprise?’, Michelle asked.

‘Yes. He’s on his last tour with work, and it’s a surprise for when he gets back. He doesn’t have a clue. He’ll love it’.

Lisa scanned the six puppies, looking for different personalities and characters. She spotted one, lying on its back in the corner while all the others climbed on top of each other. She smiled, watching this one puppy lying flat asleep with all the commotion surrounding it. Michelle leant in and picked up the sleepy ball of fur. She handed the puppy to Lisa, cupping her hands tight, making sure she didn’t drop it. Lisa felt the long floppy ears and soft hair tickle her hand. Lisa held it close to her chest. The little puppy opened its eyes slowly and gave a wide yawn, then rested its head against her and slowly drifted back to sleep.

‘This one’s sleepy, isn’t it?’.

‘That’s a girl, that one’, Michelle replied.

‘Perfect!’ Lisa announced, slowly stroking the puppy’s head. ‘When will she be ready for me to collect?’

‘After six weeks, they’ll be fully ready to go. You want this one, then?’

‘Yes. Yes, this one is perfect’.

Lisa kissed the puppy on the forehead and returned it to the pen. She smiled, looking forward to having a dog in their life. The puppy stared up at her before stumbling into the pile of its brothers and sisters.

'Well, you give me a call when you're free to collect, any time after the 28th'. Michelle ordered.

'Will do, and thank you very much'.

Lisa walked back to her car, happy that in six weeks there would be a 'little bundle of joy' running around the house, but sad that she had to wait that long. She wanted her now.

CHAPTER 4

Richard felt the air disappear from above his head, as though a vacuum cleaner had sucked it away. He was kneeling in a dried-up riverbed with two-foot-high banks on each side. Bullets penetrated the bank behind him, making little explosions in the mud, sharp stones sprayed his back. Holding his C8 assault rifle tight into his shoulder, he looked down the magnified scope as he searched for the firing point. Buildings with several broken windows lay in front of Richard and his team, amongst them alleyways criss-crossed each other. Traffic screeched to a stop and turned round when the drivers realised what was going on. The smell of unsettled dust filled the air, distant shouts echoed along the street and out into the rural fields that surrounded.

Suddenly, a large bang and the sound of bending metal echoed between the buildings. Another Rocket Propelled Grenade hit a garage door a couple of metres to Richard's right. Glancing up, he followed the trail of the rocket back to a top-floor window, open wide with curtains pulled back. Bingo! The firing point. They had been in this fire fight for nearly twenty minutes now. Richard pressed his radio:

'2-1 Charlie, this 2-1 Bravo, stand by for target indication'.

'2-1 Charlie, send when ready', came the reply over the crackly radio.

'2-1 Bravo, 120 metres, red house with blue door, three windows across top floor, roger so far?'

'2-1 Charlie, roger'

'2-1 Bravo, top left-hand window open. RPG firing point. Over'.

He let go of his radio and silence fell. The tension increased. He lifted his rifle to look through the scope. A four-man team inched along the wall of the red house on the further down the street. The men reached a blue door and spread themselves out into position. It was like a choreographed dance, everyone knew their place and when to go. One of them pushed the door open and they disappeared inside.

Richard watched the window for signs of movement. Time seemed to slow down into a dream-like state, always the most dangerous part of any mission. A few moments later, the four men returned with a skinny middle aged male. He wore dirty jeans and a T-shirt that looked as though it had not been changed for the past three months, stained with oil and grease. He was handcuffed and blindfolded.

Two 4x4 Mitsubishi Shoguns arrived on the scene, skidding to a halt. The arrested male was piled into the back seat, and the first car sped off. Richard climbed into the seat next to the driver of the second car. He removed his helmet so his head could breath in the blistering African sun. They had been out since before sunrise, trying to be fully embedded in the town before people were awake.

Now, back to the patrol base to write up the reports, call home and get some food. As soon as they were though the gates, Richard knew he could relax a little. He showered off the sweat and red dirt, his mind wandering through times spent with his perfect princess. He had been in South Africa for four months and he was starting to miss Lisa a lot. The time away was taking its toll.

CHAPTER 5

The alarm clock flashed 7:32am, the digital date showed it was the day to collect the puppy.

Lisa always wondered what Richard had eaten for breakfast while she was having hers. It would be 9:30 o'clock in the morning for him in South Africa. She hoped he would have a good day, but she knew the dangers of his job and the risks he had to take. He never spoke to her about all that, wanting to protect her.

She put the cereal bowl in the dishwasher and headed upstairs to get ready. She splashed cold water on her face to wake up, the chill making her shiver, and stared into the bathroom mirror, but her baggy eyes showed how tired she was. Grabbing the towel and drying her face, she went to her dressing table – a mirror with bright spotlights around it like that in a theatre dressing-room. She sat down and put on her make up, gradually becoming more awake.

Her mobile phone buzzed into life as a text came through.

'Love you way too much xxx'.

Just reading that boosted her energy and brought a smile to her face.

Richard stood at the table in the operations room. The noise of fans spinning on maximum speed flooded the stuffy space. Dust particles circulated in the air. His team trooped in slowly with mugs of coffee for the after-action debrief. Multi-camouflage trousers, long-sleeved shirts, desert boots, pistol strapped to their right leg. The team found their seats around a large wooden table in the centre.

Maps had been laid out and taped down; mugshots of suspects were pinned to the wall, with string leading to photos of their cars, the houses they used, the people they knew. This was a 'spider diagram' of the people whom the team called the hit list – people the South African militia was hoping to arrest in its war against the insurgents.

Richard swept his eyes around the room, counting people to check everyone was there.

‘Good ping that, Ginge’, a voice announced from across the room, referring to Richard spotting the bloke in the window.

Richard cracked a smile: ‘Well, one more terrorist tourist on their way to the holiday camp’.

Everyone in the room knew the holiday camp was a South African prison.

‘Good result today, lads, but let’s not wait until the RPG is skimming my head before you actually get the bloke’.

Laughter rippled around the table.

Lisa typed the last words of an email before finishing early. It had been a busy morning as usual. She pressed send, closed down her computer and gathered up her bag. It was 12:30pm on a Thursday afternoon, and she was in a rush, not because she feared being late, but because she was too excited to wait any longer.

‘See you tomorrow’, she said to Beth, her PA. Beth was straight out of college and a keen worker.

‘Have fun’, Beth said cheekily, suspecting a date was on the cards.

Although it was mid-August, the weather had turned cold and grey. Rain descended in frequent cloudbursts, drenching the pavements. People on their lunch breaks scurried between doorways to escape the rain and wind. Cars surged like speed-boats through sheets of water on the roads.

Lisa buttoned her raincoat and walked briskly along the pavement, her heels clicking on the hard surface, dodging large puddles, until she reached her car, a welcome relief from the cold rain.

An hour later, Lisa was parking in the same spot as she had done six weeks before. She rushed to the house to collect her new puppy as soon as possible. Michelle opened the door, grinning.

'Hello again, Lisa'.

'Hello! How's my little girl?'.

They stood in the kitchen while Michelle prepared the paperwork. Lisa signed the documents, then scooped up the golden puppy. She had grown and was more responsive to her surroundings.

Only three puppies were left to find homes. They clambered around the pen, letting out small puppy barks and yelps as they played. The mother licked each one in turn, cleaning and grooming them carefully.

Lisa scooped up her puppy, feeling her little heartbeat. She reached into her bag and pulled out a silver dog tag in the shape of a dog bone and clipped it to her collar. There was an instant connection between them.

Michelle smiled.

'Another puppy going to a caring home', she said happily.

She could tell Lisa and Richard were going to adore this puppy and spoil it rotten. Watching Lisa hold the tiny thing was like watching a mother hold her new-born baby.

Lisa threw her bag over her shoulder, wrapped the puppy tight in a towel and made her exit. There was a small crate on the back seat of the car, filled with soft blankets and toys to occupy her on the way home. The puppy played with the little teddy Lisa had given her, then fell asleep, curled up, ears flopping down as she slept, the smallest of snores fluttering out.

The team took their seats and got out their notepads.

'Right, lads! Let's get on with it. Today we managed to get a hold of Objective Fallen Basket', Richard announced. He walked over to the spider diagram and, with a marker pen, drew a big black cross through one of the photographs.

They discussed the day – what went right, what could have gone better, where they needed to go next. Each man studied various documents, trying to get a feel of the next plan. It was an official meeting, but with a hint of enjoyment. These lads loved this type of work, and when they had managed to arrest someone it lifted everyone's spirits.

Richard had started to discuss the next target of interest, but his mobile phone's ringtone vibrated it across the table as though it was trying to run away. He glanced down and saw the call was from a British number he didn't recognise, so rejected the number.

'Sorry about that. Right, where were we?'

The room had a relaxed feel: the odd joke and comment thrown around while they deliberated over papers with the headed 'Secret', half-empty coffee mugs on the table.

Minutes later, Richard's phone repeated its tune and escape attempt.

‘Same number’, Richard thought, a sales call or advertising. ‘Bane of my life these advertising calls’.

He cancelled the call again and continued his brief. The phone faded to sleep.

Twenty minutes passed and the team finished their meeting about the next job. Everyone filtered out of the room in pairs, chatting among themselves.

Richard stayed behind, signing paperwork in the now quiet room. He flicked through the pages, his eyes feeling heavy, becoming harder to stay awake with each blink. Suddenly, his phone woke him from his trance, breaking into its tune and jig once more. He glanced at the screen to see the same number displayed. His mind raced through a mental phone book, trying to recognise the number, knowing it would not be a cold caller this time.

He picked up the phone and pressed answer, tilting his head to wedge the phone on to his shoulder while he continued signing papers. A calm female voice spoke formally.

‘Hello, is that Richard Gartner?’

‘Yes, speaking’

‘I’m Susan Outreach, the chief family liaison officer at Dorset County Hospital’.

Richard's blood drained from his face. He leapt up from the desk, dropped the pen and grasped the phone tight against his ear.

Clearing a lump from his throat first. 'How can I help you?'

Richard feared he already knew the answer. He thought of a thousand different scenarios in the space of a second, but none of them measured on the scale of what he was about to hear.

The soft voice spoke again with a note of compassion.

'I'm afraid I have some bad news for you. Your wife has been in a serious car accident'.

Before she finished the sentence, Richard rushed out of the briefing room. Almost crushing his phone, he listened to every word.

'How serious is it?'

'I'm afraid it is life-threatening'.

Outside in the now fading sunlight, gasping for air, feeling as though all the life had been sucked out of him, he closed the phone abruptly and ran across the courtyard into his OC's office.

Major Nixon looked up in surprise from behind his desk. Nobody ever stormed into his office without knocking.

He stared at Richard with annoyance.

'How can I help you, Sergeant?'

Richard stood in the centre of the room, trying to gather his thoughts. The room was bright with spotlights, he could feel the heat from every single one, his face red and flushed with panic.

'Sir. I need to get home, like NOW'.

'And why is that, Sergeant?' Nixon threw back.

'My wife, my wife has been in an accident, sir. I need to get home now'.

'Oh. Serious?'

'Sir, very serious. I need a flight now. Please'. He clasped his hands together to stop himself shaking.

'OK. Go pack your bag, I'll see what I can do'.

Richard ran out of the office, bouncing off the walls, slamming into each turning as he rushed to his room. He grabbed his bag from underneath the bed. Clouds of dust filled the air. Eyes swelling with tears, nose running, his whole body shook with the fear of losing Lisa. Clothes, phone, passport, money – the bag was packed and ready in minutes. He sprinted back to the office, high on adrenaline.

Major Nixon was just finishing a phone call.

Richard stood in a sweaty mess, perspiration running down his face, patches seeping through his thin shirt. He was panting and shaking.

'I got you a flight out of SA in five hours. A military plane will drop you back at our unit. How's that?'

Richard knew he wasn't going to get much better than that

'Perfect, thank you'.

He held out his hand to shake the OC's as a gesture of appreciation. Major Nixon shook hands and, with a rare sensitivity, leaned across to squeeze Richard's shoulder.

'Go get yourself home, mate'.

CHAPTER 6

Lisa was pulling out of a junction when the right side of her car was struck by a speeding motorist whose van skidded sideways through a wet slick of mud. Screeching tyres, groaning metal and shattering glass echoed around the hills. Her car was shunted across the road and pinned against a road sign with such force, the posts collapsed and crushed her underneath.

Drivers stopped to offer assistance, but couldn't help. In a while, the sound of sirens brought some hope. The fire brigade cut Lisa from the wreckage. The ambulance crew took over immediately. The puppy lay shaking and terrified in her crate on the back seat, not understanding what had happened, her lungs straining as she barked as loud as she could.

Dorset County Hospital. Nurses rushed a stretcher down the corridor towards emergency surgery, their shoes squeaking on the laminated floor.

Lisa lay under clean white sheets, but her face was covered in dust and dirt. Her blood-stained blouse had been cut open, and pipes of fluid and blood ran from her mouth and arms like a spider's legs. While the nurses collected the right equipment, the doctors took over, storming through the double doors of surgery, using the stretcher like a battering ram.

Richard sped through the patrol base gates in his armoured vehicle, its tyres screeching on the tarmac. He straightened the steering wheel and steered with his knees while frantically dialling the hospital. The over-revving engine sounded like a swarm of bees as he swerved between slow moving cars, his phone pressed between shoulder and ear. The setting sun turned the sky bright orange. He rocketed into the airbase, knowing he had to be home before that sun rose again.

At last aboard the C130 Hercules military plane, Richard couldn't stop fidgeting. He sat on the netted seat and fastened his seat belt quickly, hoping that would get him home quicker. The tension almost strangled him as he rocked back and forth.

He sent a text to Lisa, a last-ditch effort.

'Love you, hang on, please'.

He knew deep down she wouldn't read it.

The engines turned slowly and the aircraft started to shake and vibrate. It lifted off the South African runway and into the darkened sky. Richard leant back, knowing there was nothing he could do to make it go any faster.

Lisa lay on the operating table while doctors worked on her injuries. Large spotlights on extendible arms bathed her body in harsh light. IV bags, blood bags, pipes all fed into her arms and hands. An oxygen mask covered her mouth and nose, strips of tape held her eyelids closed. The constant beeping of the heart monitor registered she was coping with the surgery. It was half past eight at night and everyone knew it was going to be a long night.

The aircraft rattled at full speed, shaking all the seats. Richard stared in a trance, not speaking or showing any emotion, a lifeless form in a live body. He prayed that Lisa was recovering during these endless hours out of contact. He knew the pilots would do all they could to get him home quickly, but would that be enough?

Every hour or so, an RAF steward updated him on where they were and if they were still on time for their arrival. The eight-hour flight felt like twenty-eight. At last, she half-jogged towards Richard.

'We're twenty minutes away from base'.

He would call the hospital as soon as they landed.

The plane banked hard left, the pitch of its engines changing to a lower note as they started to descend towards the airstrip.

With his bag between his knees, he got his things ready to leave at once. Car keys and phone in hand to gain those valuable few seconds.

A shout came down the plane.

'Five minutes to landing'.

After a loud bang, a sudden shock vibrated through the frame of the aircraft, followed by a screech of rubber on tarmac as it bounced along the runway. Everyone apart from Richard braced themselves as the engines worked at full reverse speed, slowing the plane that had landed too fast. Richard had already undone his seatbelt and grabbed his bag. He was waiting at the door before the plane had parked.

He had sudden visions of Lisa – first date, holidays, their wedding day when he watched her walk down the aisle in her white dress, hair pinned up, a huge smile, looking beautiful.

The plane stopped, the steward pulled open the door, Richard sprung from his dream and leapt down the steps, then ran across the tarmac towards the car park.

Beeps sounded as he disarmed his car alarm from metres away. The driver's door handle was stiff from being unused for months. He chucked his bag over to the passenger seat, jumped in, fastened his seatbelt as the car sped off. Through the camp gates, stones exploded into clouds of dust behind him while the guards stared after this maniac driver.

The operating room was silent now and empty. The surgeons and nurses had done all they could.

Lisa lay in a room, her eyes closed, breathing through a tube while machines monitored her constantly. A green line scrolled across a screen, beeping acknowledgment of her heartbeats. One of the nurses popped in at intervals to make sure the readings were in order, changing the drip bags when needed, flicking through the checklist at the end of the bed to make sure everything was kept up to date.

Outside, signs of dawn, orange streaks across the low skyline. Traffic starting to build up as people went about their everyday journeys. Inside, nurses and doctors arrived for their shift, fresh from their night of rest, discussing which patients were being treated and what had happened during the night.

Suddenly, the silence of Lisa's room was replaced by screeching alarms. Nurses hurried in and one of them lunged at the red emergency button on the wall. Two doctors sprinted in and took control. Lisa's internal injuries were not recovering as expected. Tension was high; the temperature seemed to jump fifteen degrees, as though an oven door had been opened. The medics trying their hardest to revive her, as the reading on the heart rate machine slowed and became weaker: 26bpm, 24bpm, 21bpm.

Richard's car screeched into the hospital car park. He had been awake for twenty-eight hours, but his nerves were fired up, adrenaline surging around his body. He sprinted into reception and pushed to the front of the queue.

'Lisa Gartner, what room?', he snapped.

The young receptionist flinched at this, but flicked rapidly through her papers.

'Room 432, fourth floor, turn left, third door on the right'.

He was already halfway down the corridor before the receptionist had finished. His shoes screeched on the polished floor. People grabbed their partners and children out of the way as he approached at full speed with no sign of slowing down.

Sprinting up the stairs, no time for elevators, two steps at a time towards floor four, he looked up to see a large number five. Hell!

A high-pitched tone pierced the air as the heart rate machine showed a flat green line scrolling across the screen.

The group surrounded Lisa's bed, heads hung low with misery, faces drained

Richard jumped eight steps down to the landing, turned and jumped the other eight to floor four, and crashed like a juggernaut into Lisa's room. The door hit the wall so hard that flecks of plaster and paint crumbled on to the floor.

'I'm Lisa's husband', breathing hard, sweat dripping down his face.

He scanned the room and saw the heart rate machine with its flat green line. He felt as though he had been hit by a wrecking ball. His legs gave way and he dropped to his knees. The doctor knelt down and held Richard's shoulder.

'I am so sorry. Your wife had too many injuries to keep her alive'.

Richard collapsed to his knees from pure exhaustion as his life collapsed in front of himself.

CHAPTER 7

Thirty-six hours had passed since Lisa had died, seconds before Richard could reach her. She had been moved to the mortuary, but he stayed in her room, unshaven, unwashed, without any food since leaving South Africa. The room was completely calm, but he was falling apart inside. His eyes were swollen and red, tear marks on his cheeks. He felt completely empty. The life he had known for the last twenty-four years had vanished like a magic trick. He could smell Lisa's perfume, it paralysed him in his chair, imprisoned him in a trance of memories.

A nurse entered the room slowly and crouched beside him, placing her hand on top of his. The gentle touch was a comfort, but he didn't flinch or move his gaze from the clouds outside the window.

'Mr Gartner, we need this room for another patient. Can I help you get your belongings?'

Richard stood slowly, his legs felt weak, his feet dragged, he looked completely drained. He walked out of the hospital, speaking to nobody and with no idea of where to go or what to do.

The clean fresh air cooled his face and he breathed deeper, his thoughts gradually becoming clearer. He would go home and tell people what had happened.

He drove home in a trance, not feeling anything, but a split-second after entering his house, the misery hit him again and he collapsed in the hallway. Head in his hands, he broke into heaving sobs. He had imagined coming home from his last tour, seeing Lisa and holding her, knowing they were together again in their own world.

'Now what? Now what do I do?'

His phone rang and he dragged himself up.

'Mr Gartner? PC Pile speaking from Dorset police'.

'Hello'.

'We are very sorry for your loss. When you are ready, of course, please could you come to the station to collect your wife's belongings.'

'OK. I'll come tomorrow'

He hung up and climbed slowly upstairs, feeling shattered and needing to lie down. The bedsheets had Lisa's scent. He was asleep the instant his head touched the pillow.

Richard woke from a deep sleep the next morning. Birds were singing, the bright blue sky looked endless, a light breeze swayed the leaves on the trees. He shook himself, remembering that today he had to collect Lisa's belongings from the police station. It was going to be a tough day and he took much longer than usual to get ready. He sat at the breakfast table, staring at the wall, his mind wandering into a daydream again until the morning post delivery shook him back to reality.

The roads were quiet on this early Sunday morning. Dust clouded behind slow-moving tractors, leaving a whiff of farm smell in the car. Driving in shorts and a T-shirt was a welcome relief after driving in military boots, body armour and a weapon slung by his side.

He drove in silence, but his mind was a noisy confusion.

Why was Lisa where she was at that time of day? Why wasn't she at work?

She hadn't told him about any appointments, or that she was taking any time off. He trusted her one hundred percent and knew she would never do anything dodgy. He just couldn't figure it out.

He arrived at the police station and took a deep breath in. He would get the full story about the crash. He felt nervous about what he would hear, how he would react.

He was greeted at the desk by a tall, skinny male, in his early thirties with neat brown hair, a well-trimmed beard and perfectly ironed uniform.

'Good morning, Mr Gartner. I'm PC Pile. I spoke to you yesterday'.

He led Richard to a small interview room.

'Please take a seat. We have a few matters to go through and some things for you to collect, including your little girl'.

In his emotional state, Richard was slow to react.

'Little girl?'.

But PC Pile had already left the room.

There was a small table in the centre and a filing cabinet in the corner. The air conditioning blew strongly and the room grew chill. Richard suddenly had goose bumps, and the hairs on his neck stood to attention.

He stood up abruptly, the plastic chair legs scraping on the lino, and paced the room. His head was spinning, he felt heavy and sick. In spite of the air conditioning, the room temperature seemed to rise by what felt like fifty degrees. Richard was sweating. He sat down again, trying to stay calm.

What little girl was the policeman talking about? Had Lisa been pregnant before he had left for SA and hadn't said anything?

Moments later, the door opened and PC Pile brought the answer, carrying Lisa's black handbag in one hand and a small crate in the other. Richard rose to his feet again, bypassing the handbag and staring straight into the big brown eyes of the eight-week old puppy. She sat slumped in the crate, her head drooped with misery and fear. She had been taken from her mother only three days ago and already been in a car crash, moved to a police station, and was now being handed over to a stranger.

Richard emotions flipped somersaults.

PC Pile stood the crate on the table.

'Your wife was on her way back from collecting your new family member when the accident happened.

'Oh, my god. I was so confused when you said "little girl" '.

'Didn't you know about the puppy?'

'Not a clue', Richard said with a glimpse of a smile, undoing the bar on the crate.

The shaking puppy stared up at him, her eyes showing little crescents of white. He leant in and gently lifted her out. There was a soft, woolly blanket in the crate, so he wrapped her in that, holding her tight to his chest. He could feel her heart racing through the tiny ribcage, but she snuggled her head into his chest. He kissed her head gently and pulled up the blanket a bit more as she gradually gave in to tiredness and fell asleep. Richard suddenly felt a huge surge of responsibility and knew must never let anything bad happen to her again.

'Is that everything you need from me?', he asked.

'Yes, just please sign here and you'll be on your way'.

Richard leant forward to sign, and made to pick up the clear plastic bag full of items from Lisa's car.

'I'll bring the crate', said PC Pile.

Richard drove back slowly, with the sleeping puppy on his lap. He didn't want to put her in the crate again, thinking she would be scared after what had happened the last time. Twisting through the narrow Dorset lanes, he tried to think of names, but only one seemed suitable: 'Princess'.

Arriving home, he sat Princess on the sofa and emptied Lisa's bag of belongings on the floor – her purse, some toys, a few doggy treats and a couple of tins of puppy food.

He went to the kitchen and mashed the soft, smelly food in a bowl. The smell drifted through the house and hung in the air. Princess opened her eyes. He lifted her up and placed her by the food. She dived in head first and started to work her way round the shiny bowl. Her tail wagged, her ears dragging on the food as she gobbled it down. The bowl slipped on the tiled floor, moving away as she chased it around the kitchen, desperate for the next mouthful. He watched her, a parent protecting a child.

Within a couple of minutes the bowl was empty. He wiped her face with tissues, kissed her soft head, and then carried her back to the sofa. Princess spun in circles to get comfortable, tucked her legs under and placed her head on the edge, watching everything he did.

He started to go through Lisa's things. Among the various cards in her purse was one for Michelle's Puppy Breeding. He dialled the number.

'Hello', a voice answered brightly.

Richard cleared the lump in his throat.

'Hello, I'm Richard Gartner. My wife Lisa bought a puppy from you last week'.

'Ah, yes. Lisa. How is everything? Do you like your surprise?'

Richard tried to gather his emotions.

'Lisa was involved in a very bad car crash on her way back from you. She didn't pull through. Your puppy is OK, though'.

The silence on the other end of the phone spoke a thousand words. Michelle gathered her emotions.

'Oh my god, really? Um. I am so sorry to hear that. Is there anything I can do to help?'

'I just need to know what I need to do', Richard said, in a muddle.

'If you think it's not the right time, I'll take the puppy back and refund you.'

'No', Richard said quickly. 'I'll keep her, but what do I need to do?'

'I'll email you all the information you need, Mr Gartner. I'm so very sorry'.

Richard stared at Princess who was fast asleep on the sofa. Curled up in a little ball, she snored gently, her stomach rising and falling. He suddenly felt completely drained, exhausted after so many stressful events. The agonizing flight from SA, the terrible time in the hospital, the bleak visit to the police station. A tsunami of misery and exhaustion crashed over him.

After what felt like a few seconds, he woke up, his eyes puffy from sleep. Princess was tucked up under his neck. Seeing the clock, he realised he had been asleep for three hours.

CHAPTER 8

Long rays of sunlight pierced the church windows, highlighting the dust floating under the high ceiling. Richard sat on the cold pew, knees clamped together, hands clutched, head high, his body numb. Guests filtered in slowly, whispering to each other. People avoided eye contact. They knew Lisa's death had crushed Richard into a wall, but nobody knew how to help.

When the church was full and silence fell. He turned round, looking for one person only, someone who should be there, one hundred percent, without question – Lisa's father, Stuart. Having scanned all the faces, he realised Stuart's was not one of them.

Richard secretly hated Stuart. He was a useless father, he had never helped or visited Lisa. She had always struggled with her feelings towards him, and their relationship was non-existent. But Richard still thought Stuart would be at his daughter's funeral, to acknowledge her and her tragic death.

The large double wooden church doors creaked open. Six men carried the dark oak coffin down the church aisle. People started crying as the coffin passed each pew, a Mexican wave of emotions. Lowering the coffin onto a stand by the altar, the bearers returned to the back of the church. Richard stared straight ahead.

The vicar, in his black surplice, made eye contact with Richard to reassure him, and as he spoke, his voice caught everyone's attention.

Richard let out a sigh he had held for the past half hour. He was used to funerals, people he worked with getting killed in action, but this one was a million times worse. He had tried to believe she had not suffered, but there was this constant aching sorrow he felt.

The choir began to sing the first hymn and people stood to join in. Deep male voices, gentler female ones, strove to match the well-rehearsed choir. Richard stared at the hymn book, remembering all the fun times he and Lisa had shared. When the singing had ended and people were sitting down again, the vicar asked him if he would like say a few words. Richard knew everything he wanted to say but thought it best to keep it between him and the grave.

After more songs and readings, the service ended and people filtered outside, gathering around the grave in the churchyard. At the head of the grave, a beautiful granite headstone stood tall, inscribed 'In loving memory of Lisa Gartner'. The vicar read the service and the coffin was lowered into the ground. Richard's heart felt as heavy and dark as the coffin in the grave.

He took a handful of earth and threw it on to Lisa's coffin. At last, a torrent of tears streamed down his face. He tried staring through them, as though underwater, but the first thud of earth hitting the coffin made him jump. He watched as Lisa's new home slowly disappeared under the earth and out of sight.

Richard was preparing to feed Princess and himself when his phone leapt into action, lighting up the dark kitchen, breaking the deep silence. His heart sank as he saw the caller's name – Stuart. Lisa's father lived miles away up country and rarely spoke to either of them. He was a drunkard who had broken contact with the family since Lisa's mum had died, fifteen years before. Richard let the phone ring out, he had no wish to speak to this distant, neglectful father.

Soon after, a voice mail alert appeared on the phone. Richard braced himself as Stuart's throaty voice bellowed down the line, blunt and to the point.

'Richard. I've heard the news. Lisa wouldn't want me there and I don't want to be there. Our lives split years ago. I don't see any reason to stay in touch. Take care'.

Stuart hung up, leaving the long dull tone of an empty line.

Richard was stunned. He never thought Stuart would be that dismissive, even of a daughter he hardly knew.

His heart started pounding and gripped the phone until his knuckles were white. Anger surged through him like a forest fire. He hurled the phone across the kitchen, feeling a sense of relief as it smashed against the wall, splitting into pieces. The relief turned to disappointment at his phone's destruction. Princess walked in, staring at him, wondering what was wrong. He realised he had to stay calm for this little puppy.

Richard sank into his bed, the silent house a blissful welcome after the funeral and Stuart's message. The gentle sound of Princess breathing, deep in dreams, was comforting. Her bed was so large it swallowed her like a log on the ocean. He got up and placed her in his bed, realising that he needed her more than she needed him. He woke next day to see Princess in the same position, snuggled against his shoulder, her warmth giving him some comfort at last.

Four weeks after the funeral, Richard, one stone lighter, his face unshaven, and looking drained, sat on the sofa with a plate of cut sausages. Princess had grown twice in size, but her puppy coat was still furry, and she was as clumsy as a new-born giraffe, with her paws still too big for her body.

'Princess, come here', he called, offering a piece of sausage.

She bounded into the sitting room, like a see-saw with two kids at each end.

'Good girl'.

She left a large slobber across his hand as she eagerly reaped her reward.

'Princess, sit'.

She slumped on the floor, waiting for another prize.

'Good girl'.

Another slice of sausage.

'Princess, paw'.

She lifted a front paw on to his outstretched hand, with a knowing look.

'Good girl. You're the best girl'.

Another prize piece.

Richard stood and picked up her lead.

'Walkies!'

It was his favourite part of the day now, time he could spend just with Princess, away from life's difficulties.

Near his house was a field leading to a large woodland, popular with dog walkers. After going through the field gate, Richard let Princess run free. She was off like a bullet, bouncing through the long grass, keen to explore every flower and tree. He walked slowly, giving her the chance to figure out what things were.

Endless blue sky, a few clouds. The warm September breeze rustled through branches, releasing the fragrant scent of leaves. Princess, still unsure of her running ability, tripped over tree roots and tired herself fast. Richard was thinking how his life had changed in just five weeks. From Lisa's terrible death to sharing his life with Princess, her final gift and the only thing keeping him sane.

They went through the wood and into another field. Princess, bouncing like a deer, headed towards a group of older dogs. She could be a little too friendly, wanting to say hello to every dog she saw, her tail wagging like a metronome on full speed. Another walker watched his dogs chasing Princess and teasing her with their superior strength. He smiled and nodded to Richard, but nothing was said. Richard walked past, slowly, in a daydream.

'Come on, Princess'.

He hated dragging her away from play but knew she wouldn't last much longer rushing at that speed. He gave her a treat and they turned towards home.

Back at the house, Princess sat while Richard rubbed a towel over her muddy fur, licking his face and nudging his shoulder. She ran inside, making a beeline for the sofa, pouncing up, spinning round, collapsing into a ball. Before Richard had made himself a drink and sat next to her, she was slowly drifting off to sleep.

He opened his laptop to write an email he thought he would never have to send. Now it was necessary. He would apply for early retirement from the army. He typed slowly, trying to choose the right words, but his eyes blurred with tears. Within one month, everything he knew – his wife, his career and a happy future were gone.

CHAPTER 9

Richard was in his office, slowly filling a box with items from a long, impressive career. Princess sat on a leather chair in the corner, head hung over the side, watching his every move. She knew he was sad but she didn't know why. She slid off the chair, walked over and head-butted his leg. He knelt down as she lay her head on his shoulder. Richard wrapped his arms around her shoulders and gently squeezed her deep soft fur covered body. He could smell the faint scent of Lisa's perfume in Princess's coat. It brought a surge of comfort over him.

Driving home, his trophies, paintings, gifts and folders piled high on the back seat, Richard felt the stress of leaving his job building up inside. He needed a release and knew what would help – a long walk in the wood with Princess. That always did the trick when he felt bad.

He pulled into a quiet car park, only one other car was there. As soon as the tyres crunched the gravel, Princess wagged her tail against the dashboard, sounding like a bass drum, and whined with excitement. Richard parked the car and opened the door. Princess bounced with joy around the open space. He smiled and immediately felt the stress levels receding.

A small figure with a bouncing puppy in tow, a mirror image of Princess, appeared on the edge of the wood. As they got closer, he saw the figure was a pretty woman in her late twenties, slim with long brown hair, brown eyes, and a piercing smile that would light up the midnight sky. She looked as though she took care of herself. A face fully made up, and not a hair out of place, even on a dog walk in the woods.

Princess stopped in her tracks and crouched like a stalking lioness, tail wagging from side to side with excitement. The other dog, a beagle puppy with ears too big for its body, hurtled straight towards her. The young woman called out as she approached.

'Sorry! He's very excitable, always wants to play'.

'Don't worry, that's all she wants to do, too. I love it when we meet friendly dogs'.

Princess chased the beagle puppy around a tree, then stopped. The beagle turned and chased her.

'How old is yours?', asked the woman.

'She's one year old now', Richard replied with a lilt of happiness, the first time since leaving for South Africa, over eighteen months ago.

'Ah, that's probably why they're both so playful. Barney's just over a year old too, the little monkey'.

She smiled and shook her head. Richard could tell she adored Barney.

The beagle lay low on his front legs, tail end high in the air, and sounded the piercing howl that only beagles do. It echoed through the wood and forced a laugh out of them both.

'He does that when he's excited and wants to play'.

'Do you walk here a lot?'

'Most of the time. It's easy to park here, and off you go. You?'

'Yes. I live up the top, so we just walk out the house and straight across the fields into the wood. It's great, and she loves it'.

'Well, my name's Emily and that's obviously Barney'. She held out her hand.

Richard stepped forward and shook Emily's hand.

'Richard, and Princess', nodding towards the bouncing golden puppy zig zagging trees, chased by a beagle.

'Princess, that's an interesting name'.

'That was my wife's nickname'.

Emily took in the 'was' thoughtfully, and didn't make any comment, but she smiled kindly. A smile that could cheer the glummest of days.

Silence followed for a short while as they watched the puppies playing.

'Well, it was very nice to meet you, Emily. I'll let you get on with your walk. Princess!', he called.

In a split second, Princess was back at his side. Blades of grass stuck in her fur and Barney's slobber was on her neck.

'Wow! She's much better behaved than Barney', Emily said and called to her puppy.

Barney sniffed around a tree, choosing to ignore her command.

Richard reached into his pocket and produced a small bag. Princess stared directly at him and sat like a statue, knowing a treat was on its way.

Smelling the aroma of beef-flavoured dog biscuit, Barney ran over and sat next to Princess, both of them waiting to be rewarded.

'Is he allowed one?', asked Richard.

'Yes, if that's OK. Thank you'.

The puppies gulped their rewards.

'Well. Again, nice to meet you, Emily, and enjoy your day!'

Richard tapped his leg to command Princess to follow him.

'And you. Take care'.

Emily took hold of Barney and put him on his lead.

After about fifty metres, Richard turned to see Emily still trying to command Barney to follow her, but he stood firm, staring down the path at Princess.

They arrived home. Princess rushed into the house and headed to her favourite snoozing place next to the sofa. Richard sighed and dumped his belongings on the kitchen worktop. He made a cup of tea, switched on the television and relaxed on the sofa, drifting into a peaceful afternoon nap. An hour later, he slowly opened his eyes to find Princess using his lap as a pillow, snoring gently.

Later that night, he switched off all the lights and went up to bed, with Princess in plodding behind. She circled on her bed. He got comfortable, then looked down and gave permission for her to join him. He knew it wasn't good practice, but he enjoyed the presence of another creature on the bed. It eased his loneliness. He kissed the back of Princess's head, like he used to kiss Lisa's.

CHAPTER 10

Princess scoffed her breakfast with gusto while Richard sat on the sofa, watching the regional news. While the newsreader shuffled his papers, preparing for the next item, headlines scrolled across the screen. 'British soldier in drunken suicide'. Richard's eyes widened instantly. He placed his coffee cup on the table with shaking hands, his stomach sinking like a falling rock. The well-groomed, smartly dressed newsreader cleared his throat.

'A British soldier on deployment in South Africa killed himself after a week-long drunken rage'.

A picture of Dave appeared, taken when he was in Afghanistan, wearing his body armour, with a weapon slung over his shoulder.

'The parents of Dave Clements have released a statement, saying their son was a loving, highly energetic soul, but unfortunately his fights with Post

Traumatic Stress Disorder and alcohol became too much for him'.

Blood rushed to Richard's face. He felt as though a hundred kilos had landed on his stomach. He tried to stand, but his legs collapsed. Kneeling on the floor, he reached for his phone, his head spinning. He had to phone Dave's mum, but his brain was empty. What would he say, how would he say anything? His hands kept shaking as he tried to press call. Eventually, a broken voice answered. Dave's mum was trying to get the energy to ask who was calling. Richard couldn't speak, there were no words. In a panic, he hung up and dropped the phone.

Memories of his friendship with Dave flashed through his mind. And questions. What happened exactly? How? Why hadn't Dave called him? What could he have done for Dave?

An hour passed. He needed to clear his head and the best way was to taking Princess for walk. Leaving the house in tracksuit bottoms, hoodie and trainers was a rare look for Richard, but the effort to get dressed properly was far too much.

They went through the gate into the field where Princess would usually leap through the grass, heading towards the wood. Today, she knew something was wrong and she stuck to Richard's side, walking slowly.

The quiet wood was soothing, the only noise from the swaying branches. Richard stared at the path, his mind racing. He would never have thought Dave could do such a thing. He had never said he was struggling, but that must have just been a front. Had Richard missed something? Had Dave ever tried to speak to him? So many questions.

They walked into a clearing where a very excitable beagle appeared, running around them in circles. Barney tried to get Princess to play, but she didn't move away from Richard's side.

'Hello again'.

Richard looked up to see Emily, her hair pulled back in a ponytail, wearing a checked shirt, jeans and wellies covered in mud.

'She doesn't seem so playful today'.

Richard's eyes were red, and he cleared his throat to speak, quietly at first, then trying again.

'I've had some bad news, so we're just walking slowly today. Go on Princess, go see Barney,' he commanded, but she didn't move an inch.

'Oh dear, I am very sorry to hear that. Is there anything I can do to help?' Emily asked kindly.

'You look very upset; do you need me to look after Princess for a few hours to give you some time to sort things out?'

'Um, I'm not sure really. I don't know what to do', he replied with a broken voice. He was struggling to process any thoughts.

'I'll take her home with me. She can run around the garden with Barney, and you can call when you've had some time to yourself'.

'That would be very helpful'.

Emily called Barney back and put him on the lead.

'We're always here, and happy to help if I can'.

Richard smiled as he began to focus on the moment.

'Let me have your number, I'll call later to collect her'.

Emily led the puppies to other side of the field while Richard walked towards home.

He entered his house, glad to be alone. Nothing he did now would scare Princess. The rage inside him was at boiling point and he punched a fist-shaped hole in the plasterboard wall. He seized a glass vase and bowled it overarm down the hall. It shattered over the wooden floor. Clenching his teeth so tight his gums hurt, he rammed open the sitting room door, grabbed the coffee table and flipped it onto its side, wrenched off the legs and kicked the wood to pieces.

After twenty minutes, the house was a wreck. Lights dangled from their fittings, glass shards from broken picture frames spread over the floors, blood was smeared on the walls.

Richard was exhausted and collapsed on the floor, covered in cuts and bruises, but the pain and release of anger was a comfort. He rolled onto his back and wiped his face. Sighing, he forced himself up, tottered to the kitchen sink and splashed cold water on his face.

'For God's sake', he mumbled.

He had been in such a rage, almost a trance, not caring about the destruction.

Three hours later, things were fairly safe for Princess to come home. He dialled the number Emily had given him. She answered in her soft, friendly voice, and offered to bring her back. Within the hour, Princess was bouncing along the hall, jumping up and begging for cuddles, licking his face with joy. Richard's problems weren't resolved, but Princess helped him cope.

Three weeks had passed since Dave's funeral, a small, intimate affair which suited his no-nonsense personality.

Richard and Princess were taking their regular walk across the field to the wood. Richard, walking slowly, his hands in his pockets, was thinking of Dave, of Lisa, his career – brooding how his life had been flipped on its head so rapidly. He looked up, but couldn't see Princess anywhere.

'Princess', he called.

No response.

He didn't worry too much. She never ran far away. A bit further along, he called out again, this time with a whistle. A gentle voice replied.

'She's over here, Richard'.

He found Emily and the puppies on the other side of an overgrown cluster of bushes. She smiled and said the friendly hello that only Emily seemed to know how to say.

Richard smiled back.

'Hey. How are you?'

'Very well, thanks. Princess just wanted to keep playing'.

'How are you feeling now', Emily asked gingerly.

'Still tender, but time will heal, I hope'.

They walked on and, for the next hour, while the puppies ran about, Richard explained what had happened. Emily listened sympathetically, wishing she could help him.

They reached the edge of the wood. Richard forced a smile.

'Sorry for telling you all this, spoiling your day'.

'Don't be silly, I'm happy to help, even if it's just listening'.

Touching his arm.

'Please let me know if you need help with anything'.

'I'll be OK, but thank you. It'd be nice to meet up for walks, let Princess and Barney play together'.

'Yes absolutely, just let me know', Emily smiled.

CHAPTER 11

Thc alarm buzzed, vibrating around his bedside table. Richard struggled to open his eyes, they felt as though clamped shut. His head weighed a thousand kilos, his brain ached in a shrunken skull. He struggled up from his pillow. When he did open his eyes, the light shot a spike of pain through his head, forcing him straight back on the pillow. He lay there for a while until he felt he could get up.

Walking slowly downstairs to make to make breakfast, Princess following close behind, a blow like a sledgehammer hit his head. His knees buckled and he crashed to the floor. Princess panicked, running up and down the hall, barking wildly.

Richard lay on the floor, stroking Princess with the little strength he could muster. Eventually, he dragged himself onto his knees, grabbing the banister to help him get up. He stumbled into the kitchen and collapsed on a chair. That short distance had made him breathless and dizzy.

'What the hell is going on?'

He sat for a while at the kitchen table, his head in his hands. Princess sat quietly, staring up, her head tilted to one side. After twenty minutes, Richard decided he had to move, do something, anything. He forced himself up and, grabbing any surface he could, slowly navigated towards the draining board to fix Princess's breakfast. The clatter of her bowl on the metal seared through his ears, a knife twisting into his skull. He managed to lower Princess's bowl to the floor, then staggered up, found two painkillers to nearly choke on, and crawled back upstairs.

'I just need some fresh air', he thought.

After what seemed to take all morning, Richard managed to get dressed. He wanted to make sure that Princess got a walk, and he had found a pair of sunglasses which helped when they got outside. Each step took one hundred times more energy than normal. Princess knew something was wrong, she slowed to match Richard's snail's pace. Twenty minutes later, they were back home. Richard went into the sitting room where the curtains were still closed. The darkness was soothing. He collapsed onto the sofa.

Princess was barking incessantly. Richard started awake. The clock on the far wall showed half past six.

'No way, that must be wrong'.

But it was right. He had slept all day.

'I never sleep like that'.

He was annoyed the whole day had been wasted, but his terrible headache had receded and the light no longer hurt his eyes.

By ten o'clock, he was feeling tired again and ready for bed. Convinced he wasn't going to sleep all night after sleeping all day, he closed his eyes, but within seconds he was asleep.

After what felt like minutes, let alone hours, Richard was woken by the alarm buzzing in his ears. Again, his head felt as though it had been squashed into half its size. He lifted himself up from the pillow. Princess looked up, hoping for a better day than yesterday.

Richard couldn't make out the pattern of the duvet, or even see the other side of the room. His sight was so fuzzy.

'Not again!'

Richard looped Princess's lead around a post outside the doctor's surgery. She had never been here before, but she sat watching the passers-by, tail wagging every time the surgery door opened, hoping it would be Richard.

Richard went in to see the consultant. The room smelt clean and fresh, and a faint light sliced through part-open blinds. He was greeted by a well-dressed man of about sixty, tall and slim, with thick grey hair and a kind face.

Dr. Peterson peered over his spectacles.

'So, Mr Gartner, what seems to be the problem?'

'Well... I woke up yesterday with a terrible headache, then completely blacked out after I went downstairs. I had the headache all day, so I had an early night, but it's still there this morning, and my vision is really blurry too'.

The doctor scribbled something on a notepad.

'Anything else?', he asked in a concerned voice.

'Well, my head feels like it's in a vice, and shrinking like there's loads of pressure on it'.

Dr. Peterson consulted a weighty hardback book.

'Right. Hop up on the couch and tell me what numbers you see on this board'.

Richard blinked, trying clear his vision, but he suddenly felt as though he was falling into a dark hole. He tumbled off the couch and landed with a thud on the floor, arms and legs in a tangled heap. The doctor shook Richard's shoulders, calling his name. Gargling sounds came from Richard's throat. His eyes were wide open but didn't seem to see anything. Dr. Peterson ordered reception to call an ambulance.

Richard slowly became aware of being in what seemed like a small box rocking from side to side. He could hear an ambulance speeding along, its siren blaring constantly. A paramedic stood over him, wearing a mask.

'Are you OK, Mr Gartner? How are you feeling?', her muffled voice asked.

With a wave of panic, Richard remembered what had happened, and realised where he was.

'Princess', he choked

'I'm sorry?' She leant closer.

'Where's Princess? My dog. She was outside the surgery.'

He fumbled wildly for his phone, ripping the intravenous tube from his arm.

'Mr Gartner, you must lie down.'

'I've got to get my dog! Please can you find my phone'.

The paramedic passed it to Richard who punched in Emily's number, then stared wildly until it buzzed in his clenched hand.

'On my way now', she replied after Richard had garbled what had happened.

Richard was wheeled along the bright corridors of Dorset County Hospital. The stretcher's wheels and nurses' shoes screeched on the polished floor. Memories of the last time he'd been there came crashing back – his panic to find Lisa and the heartache of her dying. Then his phone buzzed with a selfie photo of Princess and Emily together. He almost fell off the stretcher with relief.

Within minutes of arriving, a young doctor was by his side, checking the information sheet. A second doctor, older and portly, arrived. His face became serious as he quietly discussed the situation.

'Right, Mr Gartner, we're going to perform a CT scan on your brain to see what's causing the problem'.

Before Richard had a chance to ask anything, he was on his way back along the screechy corridors of whiteness. He was pushed into a dimly-lit room and transferred to a special bed. An array of computer screens glowed and hummed. Before leaving the room, a medic keyed in a code and a buzzing sound started. The bed slowly moved Richard head first into what looked like an endless tunnel. Richard felt he was spinning through space.

After what felt like hours, the medic returned and Richard was trundled along a different corridor to a small ward. All the doctors had vanished. Why weren't they telling him anything? A red cord hung by his side in case of emergency, his only connection to the outside world.

Later that evening the portly doctor came in, a brown folder under one arm. Richard could tell he was preparing to deliver bad news in the best possible way. The doctor pulled up a chair and opened the folder on his lap. Richard took a deep breath in and out.

'Mr Gartner, the CT scan has revealed a tumour in your brain. That's the reason for your headaches, and the sensitivity to light and blacking out. I'm very sorry to tell you the tumour is more than likely incurable, but we do have treatment which will delay the effects and ease the pain'.

Richard listened to the doctor, the hairs on the back of his neck standing to attention like the guards outside Buckingham Palace. Blood rushed to his face, his body was burning hot. He pulled his gown away from his neck to let in some air and cool down. Thoughts scattered like pieces of a jigsaw. How? What? Why? His first concern was Princess. He had promised himself he would give her a good life after a traumatic start. Would he still be able to walk and play with her, his only happiness since Lisa had died?

The doctor left the room, and a friendly nurse came in.

'We're keeping you in overnight to run some tests and keep an eye on you'.

Richard texted Emily to check Princess could stay. The puppies would be happy playing together and getting spoilt with treats.

The next morning, the same nurse came in to check the clipboard attached to the end of the bed. He flicked through the papers, glancing up at monitors and adding the readings and some notes, then looked up, smiling.

'So, looks like you're good to go home. Your stats look OK for the time being'.

Emily was sitting on the wall outside Richard's house when the taxi drew up and he got out. Wild with excitement, Princess leapt up and down, tail whipping from side to side, barking shrilly. Richard knelt down so she could put her paws on his shoulders and lick his face with vigorous attention.

'Would you like a tea or coffee?', he asked.

'Tea, please', she smiled.

Sitting at the kitchen table, with Princess still racing around the house, Richard lent back in his chair and wiped his face.

'Thank you so much, you've been a life saver. It's not often I ask anyone for help, but I needed it and you were there', he said.

It was strange talking like this to someone he didn't really know. Lisa had been the only person he could easily talk to about his needs.

'I'm always happy to help, and Princess gets on so well with Barney, it's good for him'.

She paused, then asked, 'You don't have to tell me the details, but are you OK?'

He stroked Princess's head and leant forward, taking in a deep breath.

After Emily had been told, he reached for the bag he had brought home and emptied it on to the table. Various containers and packets of pills rattled and scattered across it.

'I have to take all these.'

Emily looked shocked, her mouth slightly ajar. Her eyes became tearful.

'Don't cry, I'll be fine. I've been through much worse'. He opened his shirt to reveal a scar that ran from one shoulder almost across to the other.

Emily gasped slightly.

'My priority is her, though', he stroked Princess's head which was lodged firmly in his lap.

'She's everything to me, the only thing I have left, the only reason I get up each morning'.

They chatted for another hour or so, and by the time Emily left, she felt confident Richard would survive. She knew he would never give up on anything. She could sense his motivation and drive for living.

CHAPTER 12

Two months had passed since Richard's diagnosis. Regular hospital visits for check-ups and tests were exhausting. He was covered in bruises from bumping into things and falling down. Richard wasn't used to this. He had always been healthy and fit, had never let anything beat him, but this was taking its toll on his body and mind.

The morning walk had really tired him out. When the post arrived, Richard braced himself. He had been waiting for news of how the doctors were planning to deal with the worsening of his tumour. After reading the formal letter from the hospital – bold logo at the top, typed but signed with a fountain pen – he slammed it on the table and gulped for breath.

'Sorry', he muttered to Princess.

The doctor wanted to assign a nurse to keep an eye on him for three hours each day, and two technicians to call in now and again. They would be able to administer the drugs, monitor his general condition and deal with an emergency. Richard knew this would drive him crazy. He didn't enjoy the hospital visits, but at least he could return home for some peace and privacy.

Sarah: short and overweight, her face melted into her body from the chin downwards. Her greasy hair was pulled back so tightly it lifted her eyebrows, making her eyes look cold and unsympathetic. She had a booming, breathy, voice and an aggressive manner. Wherever she was in the house, Richard could hear her puffing and complaining as she waddled around. Her role was to administer his medication and make daily tests to ensure he stayed within the limits specified by the doctors. Her rule was law, no messing.

Terry: Sarah's son, a lanky youth with gelled hair and facial stubble. He slunk around Richard's house, ensuring all areas were safe and the equipment worked properly. Terry hardly ever spoke and rarely made eye contact. He must have felt intimidated by Richard's military background and kept his distance.

Kris: tall and athletic, bright blue eyes in a friendly face. She spoke quietly, always asking Richard if he needed anything. She monitored the charts, typing the reports on her laptop in the study.

Terry and Kris choreographed how they would each move around Richard's house. They were responsible for their particular roles, but they both had to report back to Sarah. She was the boss and she made sure they knew that.

Princess wandered around, confused by all the faces. Sarah and Terry ignored her, but Kris was the soft touch who gave out strokes and chin tickles.

Richard's home had been invaded by big, beige machines, as ugly as a thunderclouds in a clear blue sky. Boxes of needles, drugs, gloves and other medical paraphernalia were scattered in every room.

'I need some air', Richard said.

A while later, he was in the only happy place he now had, walking Princess across the field to the wood, just the two of them. Princess walked slowly, staying close, looking up to make sure he was all right. Just walking at a slow pace drained all his energy, but it was worth it to see Princess enjoying herself.

A yelp of joy announced Barney bounding towards them, followed by Emily.

'So how are the nurses?', Emily asked with a grin.

'Well, I can't say I enjoy having them in the house. I feel like a puppet being manipulated!', he tried to smile.

It had been weeks since they last walked together. Emily noticed the changes – the slow pace, his need to rest, and Princess never leaving his side. It saddened her to see this fit man with no choice but the submit to his condition.

'Princess stays close to me now, she knows something's wrong', he explained.

They opened a metal gate at the start of a path that climbed up to the top of a low hill. They reached a wooden bench on the edge of the wood, looking over a field with views into the distance.

'This is my favourite place', Richard smiled.

They stayed there a while, enjoying the view and chatting while Princess and Barney raced around each other, having fun. It was almost like the old days.

Every morning Sarah slammed the front door, making the door-knocker bang repeatedly. She bashed through to the kitchen, dumped her bag on the table, then shouted up the stairs to make sure Richard was awake. He would stay in bed, staring at the ceiling with Princess curled up under his arm, tongue drooped out of her mouth, ears flopped like socks on a washing line.

One morning, he'd had enough of the noise that woke him up. Sighing, he struggled out of bed, into his dressing gown, and carefully edged down the stairs to the kitchen to give Princess her breakfast. She followed him closely, tail wagging happily.

'Do you have to wake me like that?'

'I'm not here to waste my time', Sarah replied sheepishly, without looking round from sorting out her medical supplies.

Her uniform strained at the seams, the smell of greasy food clinging to it.

Richard slowly edged past a phalanx of tablets laid out on the worktop. He winced with the pain in his head, a clamp tightening its grip.

'How about you take your tablets before you feed that thing', Sarah ordered.

Richard stopped in his tracks as though someone had pressed pause. The pain disappeared as adrenaline surged through him. Blood rushed to his head and he felt as though the heat had been turned up by fifty degrees. Princess stared up at Richard, waiting politely for her breakfast, became aware of the fury rising inside him.

He slammed the tin of dog food on the worktop, making the tablets leap about, and spin round.

'What did you just say?'

Knowing she had overstepped the mark and Richard wasn't the type of person to take that lightly, Sarah decided to tread more carefully, but show her dominance at the same time. Still not looking at Richard, she said slowly, as though talking to an idiot,

'Take your tablets before feeding your dog, please'.

'I suggest you get out of this house as fast as you can. Nobody speaks to me like that, and nobody speaks about Princess in that way'.

He waited for Sarah to make her next move, but the kitchen started to blur, its colours fade. His knees buckled underneath what felt like a thousand tonnes of rocks. He fell, his body ricocheting off a cupboard door, and crumpled on to the tiled floor. The sound of wrenched wood and Princess's barks echoed through the house.

Princess sprinted to the front door and back, panicking and crying for someone to help. Then she licked his face to try and wake him up. Sarah knelt with difficulty next to Richard, her tight uniform stretched over her haunches, and gave Princess a mighty shove. Skidding backwards, her paws flailing as she tried to grip the floor, Princess yelped as she crashed into the wall. Scared and in pain, she managed to crawl into the sitting room.

Terry and Kris arrived. They dropped their bags as soon as they saw Richard on the floor, and rushed over.

'What happened? What can we do, Mum?', asked Terry.

'I want you to go away, now, and get on with your work', Sarah grunted as she struggled upright.

Kris began to reply, 'But we....'

'Work NOW', Sarah bellowed and pointed out of the room.

They both walked away, looking back to figure out what had just happened.

Passing the sitting room door, Kris looked in to see Princess slumped on the floor, her eyes wide open, her head drooping over her front legs. She didn't move an inch as they walked by.

Sarah stared coldly at Richard, until he came round after a few minutes. He groaned as he pushed himself up, grabbing the table for support. He felt confused. He wasn't aware of what had caused him to fall and why a cupboard door was hanging off its hinges. He staggered to a chair and slumped over the table. Princess came bouncing in from the sitting room on hearing movement and nuzzled him, laying her head on his lap for mutual comfort.

Richard's phone vibrated across the table. A text message from Emily.

'If you ever need me for anything, just let me know. All you have to say is "Meet me at my favourite place".

Richard smiled and leant back to rest for a while, but was ambushed abruptly by the pain of Sarah jabbing a long needle into his upper arm. Her hand grasped his elbow, digging her thumb into his flesh. She pulled out the needle aggressively. Blood dribbled out. She walked off without saying a word.

The painkillers began to work their way around his body, so he shuffled into the sitting room and lay on the sofa. Kris came in to get some updates.

'I'll get you a plaster for that blood', she said gently.

'It's just a bit of blood. He's a big boy, I'm sure he'll manage', Sarah bellowed from the hall.

'Hero, apparently!', she scoffed. She had seen the framed photographs of Richard and Lisa at the ceremonies when he was awarded his medals for bravery.

Kris pressed down on the wound to stop the bleeding, smiling at Richard to comfort him. She looked over her shoulder to make sure the coast was clear before whispering,

'Sorry about her'.

'Where's Princess?', asked Richard, barely able to lift his head. The drugs were really kicking in.

Kris stood up straight, and moved away from the sofa to avoid the question. She didn't want to be the one to answer it.

Richard's eyes opened wider with alarm.

'Where's Princess?', he asked with as much strength as he could.

'Terry put her in the garden', Kris said quietly, avoiding eye contact.

He looked towards the window to see rain pouring down outside. Branches were thrashing about. He wrenched himself up from the sofa and staggered to the kitchen. Terry and Sarah were sitting opposite each other at the table, chatting.

Richard opened the door to the garden. Princess was trembling, her coat soaked and dripping, her tail between her legs. He dragged her inside, she was scared. Terry and Sarah looked away.

'Nobody comes here and treats her or me badly. This has to stop now!', Richard shouted at them.

He grabbed the kettle and hurled it across the room, his anger at breaking point. But the lights began to dim and edges became blurred. The clamp was round his head again, and again his legs crumpled and he thudded on to the floor.

Sarah carried on sipping her coffee without a care in the world.

'This wouldn't keep happening if he controlled himself a bit more', she sneered.

Terry, shamefacedly, got up and went over to Richard. Kris had heard the noise and came in from the study.

'What on earth happened?', she demanded, a change from her usual gentle manner.

She knelt down at Richard's side and cradled his head in her lap.

'Is someone going to tell me what happened?', she asked again, still angry.

'Go home! That's you done for the day', Sarah yelled at them both, pointing to the front door.

'But...'. Kris could hardly speak.

Terry shuffled his feet, torn between obeying Sarah and feeling guilty.

'Both of you, now!'.

The front door slammed behind them. Terry scarpered, but Kris stayed, wondering what to do next. Who could she report this to? Who would believe her?

After a few minutes, Sarah barged out of the door, stomped to her car and drove off.

CHAPTER 13

A strange kind of peace settled on the house. Richard's 'enemies' and kind Kris had finished their duties and been sent packing. Sarah had dragged him back to the sofa and checked his medication before she left. He laid his head back and closed his eyes. The tense atmosphere receded gradually until it all felt safer. Princess had calmed down too, she lay next to him and he could tell her heart had stopped racing.

His phone rang. Emily.

'Hey, how are you?'

'I'm OK, just feel very weak. I pass out whenever I do too much. But can't complain', he tried to add some lightness to ease the situation.

'But I'm worried about Princess', he continued. 'Sarah told Terry to shut her out in the garden this morning, in the pouring rain. She can tell there's something wrong with me'.

‘What are you going to do?’, Emily asked, her voice breaking.

‘I need to make a plan. I’m not having them treat her badly in our own home’.

They chatted for a while, then said their good-byes.

Richard was enjoying a bit of peace and quiet, but the silence was soon shattered by the front door slamming. Terry and Sarah had returned. Sarah marched into the sitting room, clutching her medical bag Terry slunk away to check his machines.

‘What are you doing back here, I told you to get out’, Richard shot up from his seat.

The rush of blood to his head made him dizzy.

‘You sit down’, Sarah stormed towards him, her mouldy, sweaty smell mingled with cigarette smoke.

She grabbed his shoulder and forced him back down. Princess had started barking as soon as they walked in. Sarah wrapped her chubby fingers around Princess’s collar and dragged her off the sofa. Shoving her into a corner and, like a footballer delivering a penalty, followed by a swift kick into Princess’s ribs. A squeal of pain seared through the room.

Richard struggled to get up, his mind in a fury. He lurched towards Sarah, but again, the room spun as he blacked out on the floor. Equally infuriated, Sarah upended her medicine bag onto the floor, filled a syringe, wrenched Richard's arm, and jabbed the needle deep into his flesh. She kept slapping his face hard to get a response, muttering curses. When that didn't work, she snatched a fistful of hair and repeatedly thumped his head on the wooden floor until one of the boards cracked.

Princess rarely barked, but the commotion was too much for her. She hurtled towards Sarah and sank her teeth into her plump forearm, biting as hard as she could. Sarah shrieked like a banshee and Princess let go. Sarah scrambled clumsily to her feet and edged away, her back against the wall. Never breaking eye contact, Princess crept forward, showing her teeth and growling. With a lunge towards the door, Sarah bundled herself out, slamming it shut behind her.

With the threat gone, Princess did her best to wake Richard. Nudging, licking, front legs on chest – nothing working. Then his head rolled to one side, eyelids flickering, legs twitching. Princess nudged her nose under his armpit and chin, barked loudly, and trotted in a circle, her claws skittering loudly on the floorboards. Richard gasped. Jumping up onto her back legs and driving down hard on the floor, she made another high-pitched bark, and stared at him to see if that had made a difference. He opened his eyes and stroked Princess's back. She leapt forward licking and sniffing his face, her low whine of pleasure music to his ears.

Richard sat up and shuffled back to lean against the sofa. Princess sat down firmly on his lap to keep him safe and stared at the door in case Sarah returned. The more awake he became, the more pain he felt – face hot and raw, scalp throbbing. He ran a hand through his hair and felt something wet. There was blood and strands of hair all over his fingers. He remembered Sarah kicking Princess across the room and quickly checked her from head to tail.

'Did she hurt you, sweetheart?'

Princess gazed up at him, mouth open wide, tail thumping with happiness.

When he felt stronger, he shuffled towards the kitchen, Princess barging ahead to make sure the coast was clear. It wasn't. Terry and Sarah were sitting at the kitchen table, having a nice cup of tea. Sarah's forearm was in a bandage. Princess blocked the doorway, growling, snarling, staring hard at her. Sarah shimmied her chair away, and reversed her large form towards a wall.

'What the hell is going on?', Richard demanded. 'I've got blood all over the back of my head, there's a crack in the sitting room floor and Princess is being very protective. Explain!'.

'That dog needs putting down, it's out of control!', Sarah whined.

Gasping and moaning dramatically, she unwrapped the bandage to reveal four red marks. Richard wasn't sure what had happened, but he knew Princess would never be aggressive in any way – unless something serious had happened.

'Why would she bite you? And why have I got blood all over the back of my head?'

'You were messing about and fainted, you banged your head on the floor when you collapsed. I just pinched your cheeks to wake you up, and that's when –' she cradled her horrible arm – 'when that beast attacked me'.

Richard looked down at Princess staring devotedly up at him. He swayed with shock, utterly not believing this could have happened. Terry had been looking at Sarah while she performed, then glanced at Richard to see if he had bought the story. Richard caught his eye. It was so obviously a set up, he could hardly believe they had the nerve to try it out.

'I will be reporting that animal to the police and I want it put down,' Sarah continued, pompously. 'You are not a well man and I can't look after you if that thing's going to attack me when I work'.

Terry was staring at his tea, not sure this ploy of Sarah's was going to work.

Trying to stay very calm in case he passed out again, Richard took several deep breaths before delivering his speech.

'You've done nothing but treat me and Princess with the utmost contempt ever since you started here. Princess has never been aggressive to me or anybody. I can remember you kicking her before I fainted. How dare you! This is her house, not yours'.

Terry sank into his chair. Even Sarah didn't respond, although she looked mutinous.

'I want you out of here now, and don't come back. Ever'.

Sarah wrapped the mangled bandages around her arm, her teeth clenched. She stomped over to the table, and kicked the chair away. The sound of clattering wood on the tiled floor added to the tension.

Richard, standing by the door, refused to be bullied, leant down to pull Princess close to avoid any further harm.

Sarah grabbed her bag and barged past him, her rugby player shoulders bouncing off the wall. He caught the stench of sweat and cigarettes. She stomped towards the front door, sounding like a herd of elephants, wrenched it open, slammed it shut. Terry tiptoed towards the door, as though hoping he were invisible. Richard was too disgusted with him to waste any words.

CHAPTER 14

Emily gently peeled away a blood-soaked towel from Richard's head. He winced as the pain shot through his whole body. She cleaned the tangled hair and bloody gash.

'I can't believe they left you like this. They're meant to look after you, not attack you', she said, angrily.

'Thank you. You're the only person I can count on now'.

'Don't be silly, anyone would help, there we go, all done'.

She flicked on the kettle and prepared two mugs for some tea.

The day had really taken its toll on Richard. His body was running on empty. His head slowly drooped as he slowly drifted off to sleep.

Emily made the puppies sit quietly on the sofa after their game of tag.

BANG, BANG. A hammering on the front door knocker shattered the calm, quickly followed by knuckles rapping on a window. Richard's eyes sprung open as Emily hurried to the door. Two large police officers stood there, feet planted firmly in case of any trouble. Emily stared in shock, unable to say anything.

Policeman No. 1 relaxed his stance, seeing who had answered the door.

'Ah. Is Mr Gartner available?', he asked, more civilly than he had previously intended.

'Yes, but he's had rather an ordeal', Emily replied cautiously. She didn't want to say the wrong thing.

'Yes, so we've heard. We'd like to have a chat with him'.

Emily stepped aside. They removed their hats and walked in.

'Mr Gartner, I'm PC Wilson and this is PC Townsend, Dorset Police'.

Policeman No.1 announced. He was six foot tall, of muscular build, clean shaven. His uniform was neatly pressed, without a single crease, shoes polished. His colleague was running to fat, his uniform straining to hold it in. His frown gave the impression he was looking for some police action to get involved in.

'We have been informed of a violent dog attack that happened here, earlier today', PC Wilson announced.

Princess bounded into the room, closely followed by Barney. She trotted across to say hello to the visitors, her tongue lolling out, tail wagging. Both policeman stepped back, taking hold of their battens for protection. Princess weaved between them, rubbing against their legs and looking up, hoping for a friendly pat. Barney jumped up to get a better view, head cocked on one side, panting with excitement.

'Oh really? If you mean that dog there, does she look violent?'

'So, what happened then, Mr Gartner', PC Townsend demanded an explanation.

Richard tried to put all the details in order, worrying what might possibly happen next.

'I have a brain tumour that makes me faint a lot when I get stressed. I used to be fit, but now just walking upstairs wipes me out. A nurse comes to give me my medication, and two others look after various things, but...', Richard paused to get his breath back and think before going on.

'But what, Mr Gartner?' PC Wilson this time.

'But the nurse is so rough and shouts at me. She treats Princess, that's my dog, horrendously, and when I do faint, I wake up with injuries that don't make sense. I don't want any of them here. We're fine on our own'. Richard's voice rose with anger and frustration.

'Well, unfortunately, Mr Gartner, your nurse, Ms Downing, has a nasty bite on her forearm and is pressing charges against you and...' PC Wilson pointed at Princess as she sat patiently, tongue lolling.

'Princess', Richard reminded him.

Emily was holding on to Barney's collar.

'That's outrageous!', she exclaimed. 'Princess has never been aggressive to anyone. That nurse was cruel to Princess and was hurting Richard. Princess was just protecting him from a bully', she blurted out in a panic.

PC Wilson was not prepared to discuss the matter further.

'Mr Gartner, you will receive a letter regarding this matter and the date of a court appearance that you will be required to attend. I'm sorry to have brought this news. We'll leave you now'.

They showed themselves out. Their footsteps were heard trudging down the path.

Richard and Emily sat in a state of shock. Princess jumped up for a reassuring cuddle, while Barney curled up on the floor. The only sound was the clock ticking.

The following day, Richard was sitting on the bench at the front of the house while Princess snuffled around the garden. There was some faint sunshine and a mild breeze.

'Are you OK, Richard?', Emily asked. She had brought Barney along to play with his friend. Barney sprinted over to Princess, ears flapping like wings.

'Yes, just having a quick snooze', Richard smiled.

He knew his condition was worsening by the day, but he tried to be happy when Emily called.

Emily perched next to Richard.

'So how are you feeling, really?'

'Exhausted, nervous, angry, confused. You name it, I feel it'.

Emily rubbed his back for comfort. The gentle touch reminded him of Lisa doing the same. Richard's head dropped wearily.

'But guilt is what I feel above everything else', Richard announced, staring down, too embarrassed to make eye contact.

'Guilt? What on earth do you feel guilty about?', she asked again, seeking an answer.

Richard sniffed and cleared his throat.

'Guilty that I wasn't here for Lisa when she died. I was the on other side of the world and I couldn't protect her. It would never have happened if I hadn't been away. She put up with me being away all the time. Worrying, waiting and then, as I've nearly finished, that happens. She never got to enjoy me being retired, at home, holidays together. And now I'm guilty again, I can't protect Princess either. I've failed! I've failed Lisa; I've failed Princess. They're the ones who have suffered for my failure, and only ones who should never have suffered'.

A tear ran down his cheek. He had never shown his emotions in public, it was something he had learnt to control years ago, but this time he had to let things go.

Emily was stunned to hear this admittance of misery. She had always admired Richard for his strength. Now, she could see what he was hiding. She felt a huge wave of sympathy for him. This man had been through so much in his life. His love for his wife was beyond measure, his love for Princess was just as strong. And after all this time, with a serious brain tumour, and the nightmare visits from Sarah and Terry, all he could think was that he couldn't protect them'.

Emily turned his face towards hers.

'Now you listen to me, Rich. You have nothing to feel guilty about. It's not your fault. None of it is your fault. From what I've heard, you were an incredible husband. You couldn't have known what would happen, and as for Princess, she has the best life of any dog I know. She adores you'.

Richard wrapped his arms around Emily's slight shoulders and squeezed tight.

'Thank you. Thank you for everything', he whispered.

'Nothing to say thank you for! I haven't done anything', Emily was reassured to have said the right thing.

'I do have something to ask you', Richard announced, leaning back on the bench. Princess and Barney were pretend fighting over a stick, each taking it in turn to run with it or chase the other.

'Anything. Just ask'.

'If anything happens to me, or when it's time for me to go...', he took a long, deep breath to steady his emotions.

'Would you look after Princess? You're the only person I trust. She already knows you, she loves you and Barney, and I know she'd have a good home and life with you'.

Before he could even finish this sentence, Emily had butted in.

'Of course! You don't even have to explain. I love Princess and I'd treat her just the same as Barney'.

'Thank you', he said with a long breath out, the weight lifting off his heart.

CHAPTER 15

Richard stood in front of the mirror, tightening his blue tie. He looked tired, his face had aged. He knew it would be a difficult day, the possibility of losing Princess was more than he could bear. A high-pitched blare signalled the arrival of his taxi. He buttoned up his jacket and left home to face the ordeal.

The magistrate's court echoed to every sound. Its sombre fittings and bland walls gave an air of authority. People knew how they were expected to behave in there. The coat of arms of Great Britain hung on the wall above the magistrate's bench. Richard made his way to where two solicitors sat talking. They didn't acknowledge his arrival. Next to them sat the menacing figure of Sarah in a grey suit, make-up and neatly tied hair. She caught Richard's eye and looked away quickly.

Richard took his seat and poured himself a glass of water from the jug on the table. His hands were shaking with apprehension. He had fought in several wars, parachuted into enemy territory, been in great danger, but the thought of hearing the worst possible verdict scared him more than any of these.

The magistrate and her assistants made their way to the front.

'All rise', said the clerk of the court.

People scrambled to their feet. Richard stood as though he were on military parade, hoping this sign of respect would help his case.

'Please sit down'.

The atmosphere in the room became tense. Sarah stared straight ahead, avoiding any eye contact with Richard. Her solicitor stood up, a tall woman in her mid-forties.

'On 5th May, my client was conducting her normal daily routine as a nurse to Mr Richard Gartner. Mr Gartner collapsed, causing my client to take immediate first aid action. While attending to Mr Gartner, my client was attacked by his dog which bit her right forearm. This has left her scarred, scared and uncomfortable in carrying out her daily tasks. This dog cannot be controlled properly due to Mr Gartner's illness. It is unfair on my client to allow this animal to continue endangering people'.

Richard had to fight not to leap up and deny each lie in this ridiculous fable that made Princess into an uncontrollable killing machine.

'Mr Gartner, do you have anything in reply to this statement?', the magistrate asked.

Richard held on to the table to help himself up.

'Yes. I would like to say that my life has been a constant struggle since my wife died in a car accident, nearly three years ago'.

His sad voice held the room's attention.

'She was everything to me. But before I lost her, she gave me the most precious gift I could ever have wished for, my dog'.

A sigh of emotion, like the pressure released from a valve, filled the room.

'Princess has kept me sane since my wife died', he continued, his voice getting weaker.

'She has absolutely no aggression in her, she has never hurt anyone or even barked out of place in her life.'

To make sure his case was clear, Richard stood as straight as he could.

'Since Ms Downing started coming to my house, she has abused me verbally, physically and mentally'. On 5th May, Ms Downing shut Princess outside in a heavy rainstorm. I told her to leave, but she returned later that day. She kicked my dog hard, and I had a fit and passed out. When I came round, there were bruises on my face and bleeding from the back of my head. These were caused by Ms Downing, not by me collapsing. I can only think that Ms Downing hurt me and that Princess did what she did to protect me'.

Richard stared directly at Sarah, his jaw clenched shut with contempt. Sarah's plump face flushed a deep red.

Tension was building. The wall clock showed it was midday, but Richard felt as though this had been going on for hours. He was drained of energy. The room was hot and stuffy, and he drifted off into a daze, his head resting on his chest.

'Mr Gartner, Mr Gartner?', the magistrate called.

Richard slumped in his chair, not hearing anything.

Sarah took this as a chance to show her nursing skills. She made her way over to Richard and placed two fingers on his neck to check his pulse.

'Ma'am, please can we take a break so I can take care of Mr Gartner?', Sarah asked the magistrate in a professionally concerned way.

'Of course, Ms Downing, we'll re-adjourn in fifteen minutes'.

Sarah leant over Richard, tenderly holding his head like a mother to her baby. She splashed his face with cold water from the jug.

'Richard, come on. Wake up now. Everything will be fine', she whispered, but loud enough for others to hear, making sure they understood how caring she was.

Richard let out a long, gargling noise as he came round. As his focus returned, he realised Sarah was standing over him, her eyes staring deep into his and smiling. She had just played the act of a caring nurse who would never do anything wrong.

Richard surged up from his seat, pushing the table away.

'Get away from me,' he said angrily.

Sarah returned to her seat.

'Thank you, Ms Downing', the magistrate said, clearly impressed with Sarah's professional behaviour.

At that point Richard knew it was all over. He'd lost the battle. He felt as helpless as when he was on that return flight from South Africa – not able to protect the most important love of his life.

It was all too much for him. He slumped his head into his hands, shoulders heaving with uncontrollable waves of sorrow. Everyone's eyes were drawn to this sight. Eventually, Richard raised his head and gritted his teeth, trying to get his emotions under control long enough for the verdict.

The magistrate spoke calmly and clearly.

'I understand Mr Gartner has had a very sad and worrying time recently. This has caused him to depend too much on the support and company his dog provides. However, I cannot allow that a dog, however loving and faithful it might be to its owner, is free to attack another individual. From what I have seen today, it is clear that Ms Downing is a competent and sympathetic nurse. But more importantly, it is a fact that Ms Downing is at risk from Mr Gartner's dog should she continue to attend to you. Therefore, I find in favour of Ms Downing and find Mr Gartner guilty of owning a dangerous animal'.

'Please! Please don't punish my dog! Ms Downing attacked me while I was unconscious. Princess was protecting me, that's all'.

'Mr Gartner, it is clear Ms Downing has your best health interests at heart...'.

Richard took a deep breath in.

'That was all an act'.

'Stop! Mr Gartner. Just stop', the magistrate held up her hand to indicate there would be no further interruptions. She continued,

'Mr Gartner, from your medical records I understand that you have a only few months to live. It would be unacceptably harsh to remove your dog from your possession at this unfortunate time'.

Richard hung on to this faintest glimmer of hope. Sarah fell back in her seat, dabbing her face and sighing dramatically.

'To that end, Mr Gartner, your dog can stay with you until the time comes. At which point Princess will be put to sleep by a vet to prevent further aggressive attacks. In the meantime you will ensure your dog is safely locked up during Ms Downing's visits'.

The expression on Sarah's face was that of a happy child on Christmas Day. She swaggered confidently out of the courtroom.

Richard sat frozen still, his mind racing with thoughts of how he could prevent this decision. The bustling hubbub of people leaving faded away until there was silence. He took a deep breath, got up and walked out, holding on to the tables and chairs for or support.

Princess bounced down the hall to greet Richard with her usual excitement and joy. He knelt down to greet her, cuddling her while she laid her head on his shoulder.

'I have failed you', Richard stammered, grief-stricken.

His whole world had crashed on rocks.

CHAPTER 16

Richard woke to the smell of sweat and cigarettes. Sarah was standing outside the bedroom door. Terry squeezed through the gap in silence to collect Princess. In the days since the court case, Sarah had become more cruel towards Richard, leaving him in bed for hours. Any sudden movement caused him acute pain. He often fell unconscious to the floor.

Terry grabbed Princess's collar and dragged her from the bed. Her legs couldn't stand quickly enough, so she crumpled to the floor with a thud. He dragged her down the stairs and out into the garden where he had built a small cage – a wooden frame with criss-cross wire fencing. The gate swung open, and Terry pushed Princess inside. She lay down in a corner, her head on her forelegs. Her eyes stared back in utter misery towards the house.

This would be the routine from now on. Richard had tried to arrange for Emily to collect Princess for her daily walk, but Sarah always refused. He could only dream of walking Princess, watching her play in the long grass, weaving between the trees and chasing the sticks he threw for her. He remembered lovely walks with Princess, Emily and Barney. And the wonderful life he had enjoyed with Lisa.

The happy images were quickly shut down like a power cut by Sarah's rasping voice.

'The mutt is fine. Don't get up.'

The seams of her uniform struggled to stay together as she wedged herself in the bedroom doorway.

'I've met a lot of really bad people in my life, but they were all fighting for a reason', said Richard.

Sarah rolled her eyes and shrugged her shoulders. She couldn't care less.

'Well, the sooner you pass away, the sooner I can do everyone a favour and take that animal to the vets for its injection.'

She smiled triumphantly, provoking Richard to react. Which he did.

'How dare you talk about her like that! Who do you think you are? Say what you like about me, but don't you ever talk about her like that', Richard screamed.

He knew what was going to happen next. The rage, followed by collapse into darkness, then returning to the misery of this nightmare.

'Don't you dare touch him, just leave him to come round on his own', Sarah ordered Terry as she reached the bottom of the stairs and headed towards the kitchen.

Weeks passed. One day, on a high with her power, Sarah stomped out to Princess's cage where she was whimpering. She picked up a large stick from a muddy flower bed and, breathing heavily, bashed it against Princess's cage.

'Shut up! Nobody cares if you're cold or hungry', she screamed.

Richard heard the commotion.

'I'll kill that monster if she hurts Princess', he thought, lurching to the window to look.

Princess was cowering in a corner of the cage, looking up at Richard's window, hoping he could help. Another crash thundered through the house as Sarah stormed back into the kitchen.

Richard lay in bed, thinking 'How has this gone so wrong? If it weren't for Princess, I'd have gone a long time ago. I can't give up on her'.

CHAPTER 17

'This is the day.' Richard knew his body was closing down for the last time. He scrabbled to get his phone and sent a text to Emily.

"Meet me at the place".

He hadn't been outside for weeks and just hoped he would make it. Moments later,

"You OK? On my way now".

Richard inched cautiously towards his wardrobe, dragged a T-shirt and jeans over his withered body, and wrestled his feet into a pair of trainers. Unused to wearing shoes, he tripped on a rug and thudded to the floor.

'Stop banging around up there', yelled Sarah, waddling out from the kitchen.

Gritting his teeth, Richard grabbed at any support he could find to wrench himself upright. He managed to wobble downstairs. Reaching the hall, he froze, hardly daring to breath in case he was discovered.

Sarah was ordering Terry around in the kitchen, so her attention was fixed on dominating somebody else for now but also meant the backdoor to the garden was heavily guarded.

Achingly slow, Richard opened the front door and edged outside, the sound of his feet on the crunching gravel was deafening. Making his way around the back of the house along the garden wall to try to get access to the garden where Princess was imprisoned. Reaching the back gate and slowly lifting the lever to open revealed a big problem, it was locked from the inside. Richards mind raced as he made a plan of attack. Mustering all his strength he grabbed the top of the wall pulling himself up, the surge of adrenaline did its job to get him up the wall but soon faded as his world went dark, as he collapsed into a muddled heap on the garden floor inside Princess cage. Landing with the sound of cracking bones.

Princess had been curled up in a corner, but leapt with joy when Richard arrived. Licking his face, her tail wagging maniacally. Richard slowly awoke but to the most amount of pain he had ever felt. The fall had done its damage on an already damaged body. Richard looked over his shoulder to make sure he had not been seen or heard from the kitchen. Unlocking the garden gate and making their way to across the field towards their favourite place, now limping and groaning with every excruciating step.

Sarah and Terry were sitting at the kitchen table. Sarah's raspy breathing through her nicotine-stained teeth formed a counterpoint to the ticking of the clock. Terry was reading a comic, but suddenly became aware of a change in the atmosphere outside. He shot out of his seat and looked outside to see the dog pen was empty, its gate open.

'The dog! The dog's gone!'

He hurtled upstairs. Richard was not in his bedroom, but his phone was.

"Meet me at the place".

"You OK? On my way now".

'He's gone too', Terry yelled down the stairs.

'What do you mean he's gone? He can't even stand up! How's he gone?'.

Terry ran downstairs and out to Princess's cage where the door swung on its hinges. He kicked it shut in frustration.

'I suggest you go to the woods and find him and his mutt and bring them back', Sarah bellowed at him from the back door.

Richard was stumbling along the path up to the bench at the top. Grabbing anything to support his bodyweight which was feeling heavier and heavier with each step. Grabbing hold of a barbed wire fence coursed his hands to bleed. Princess whined to see him in pain.

Terry reached the path into the wood, and sprinted fast, following the trail of blood as though on a treasure hunt. He was breathing heavily and sweating in his polyester uniform.

'Shit, shit, shit.' An infuriated Sarah waddled after him. She didn't want to miss any action, but couldn't keep up.

Princess walked slowly next to Richard, occasionally looking up to see the pain in his face as he gritted his teeth. Each step dragged. The climb took every last ounce of energy he had left as he reached the top a familiar feeling washed over, the light begun to fade, the crumbling of the knees as his head dragged him to the floor. As he crashed to his knees to pain shooting through his body forced a cry. Richard forced his opens biting hard on his tongue to avoid blacking out completely, he knew this was his only chance. As blood streamed from his mouth, coughing which coursed his broken ribs to take the lead in the pain competition, he forced himself back to his feet. Barely able to see where he was walking he tripped and plummeted towards the ground, cracking his head against the bench as he fell. Princess stood over him, barking in distress.

Terry stopped in his tracks to check the direction, then ran towards the sound.

'We'd best get that bloody dog', Sarah mumbled to herself, wheezing and sweating, yards behind.

Emily heard the barks and rushed up the hill. Barney shot off in an exciting race to see Princess and play like they used to. As Emily drew closer she saw the pain Richard was in, hunched over and moaning.

'Oh my God,' she screamed, seeing the blood and bruises tattooing Richard's face. She knelt beside him, aghast at his wheezing breath, blood running down his neck and bloody hands.

'We have to get you to hospital!', Emily punched a call for an air ambulance.

'No! Go and take Princess now, before they get here. Please!' Richard mumbled, struggling.

'I'm not leaving you here, you've got to get to a hospital'.

'NO! Go NOW!' He reached out for Princess, holding her as tight as he could.

'I love you girl more than you can ever know'.

Princess stared at Richard, licked his face, whimpering with fear.

Terry crashed into the metal gate in the wood below, the clang echoing through the trees.

'Go!', Richard demanded, making one last-ditch attempt to keep them safe.

Emily snapped out of her trance and snapped Barney's lead on Princess's collar.

'Come on, Barney', she called, leaving the hill by another path. Barney and Princess knew they had to behave.

By the time Terry reached the top, it looked very different from what he expected to see. Instead of an upright Richard with Emily helping him, and Princess sitting peacefully at his feet, Richard lay tangled on the ground. Emily, Princess and Barney had gone.

Terry crept towards Richard's inert body. He leant down and placed two fingers on his neck.

'Shit'.

Terry jumped up and sprinted down the path he thought Emily and the dogs might have taken. He hurtled downwards and eventually skidded to a halt on the gravel of the car park. Emily was driving away, Princess and Barney looking out of the rear window.

The metal gate clanked and, eventually, sweating and puffing, Sarah staggered up the hill, but she was too late to inflict more misery.

Richard was dead.

CHAPTER 18

Emily was singing along to some music as she drove down the winding country lane. Princess lay across the back seat, her golden coat rippling in the breeze, mouth open wide to catch the fresh air. Barney's long ears flapped gently in the wind as he watched the world pass by the window.

She parked up in front of a church whose tall tower dwarfed its surroundings. They all got out of the car and made their way along an old cobbled path to a corner of the churchyard. Scattered gravestones stood at wonky angles. Scent from the flowers placed in front of gravestones wafted through the air. Emily walked with head held high and a smile on her face, feeling proud of what she had achieved.

She sat down on a wooden bench nestled against a corner wall. Barney perched on his back legs next to her, looking over the well-kept graveyard. Princess lay with her head resting over a grassy mound, her face staring at the beautiful granite headstone.

In loving memory of Lisa Gartner.
Here in peace lies Richard Gartner alongside his wife.
He was a wonderful man who loved no-one
more than he loved his wife and his dog.

THE END…

Printed in Great Britain
by Amazon

33619360R00081